This book belongs to

♡ Jhanvi ☆

Booh

Alice

The White
Rabbit

Starring

The Cheshire
Cat

The Queen
of Hearts

The Mad
Hatter

First published by Parragon in 2010

Parragon
Queen Street House
4 Queen Street
Bath, BA1 1HE, UK

ISBN 978-1-4075-8760-8
Printed in China

Bath New York Singapore Hong Kong Cologne Delhi Melbourne

One summer day, a young girl named Alice found herself trapped with a history lesson. While her sister read of ancient kings, Alice crowned her cat, Dinah. The day was simply too splendid for lessons, thought Alice.

As soon as she could, Alice slipped away from her lesson.

"Oh, Dinah," she sighed, "in my world there would be no lessons. All would be nonsense."

As Alice dreamed of her
wonderland, a well-dressed white
rabbit ran past.

"I'm late! I'm late!" the White
Rabbit cried. Alice raced after
him. "He must be going somewhere
awfully important," Alice said to
Dinah. They followed the White
Rabbit to a rabbit hole.

Alice squeezed into the rabbit hole, even
though she knew she did not belong there.
"After all," she said, "curiousity
often leads to...TROUBBBLLLE!"

Alice's voice disappeared
into a dark hole along with the
rest of her. She floated down
through the darkness. As a lamp
drifted past, Alice turned it on and
looked about her.

"Curiouser and curiouser,"
she said.

As Alice landed, a pair of white rabbit feet ran past her.

"Oh, wait, Mister Rabbit!" she called, and ran after them, all the way to a little door. As she twisted the doorknob, a nose wriggled under her hand. What a strange place! Alice thought. She asked the doorknob if she could go through.

"Sorry." said the doorknob. "You're much too big. Why don't you try the bottle on the table?"

A glass bottle labeled 'Drink Me' appeared. With each sip, Alice shrank.

Now she could fit through, but the door was locked! Tiny Alice couldn't unlock the door. A magic cookie made her giant Alice, but giant Alice couldn't fit through the door! She began to cry, and her tremendous tears flooded the room. Alice shrank herself again, and floated through the door's keyhole in the glass bottle.

A wave swept Alice into a very odd race. Some fish and some birds ran round a dodo who was smoking a pipe. They were trying to get dry while the waves kept them wet.

Alice spotted the White Rabbit ahead of her, washed up in an umbrella on the beach.

"Mister Rabbit!" she called, and started to follow him into the woods. Instead of finding him, however, she found a pair of twins.

"I'm Tweedledee." said one. "I'm Tweedledum." said the other. Alice told them she was looking for a White Rabbit because she was curious about where he was going.

Tweedledum sighed. "It can be dangerous, to be too curious." he said.

"I'm sure you are right," said Alice, but hurried off to find the White Rabbit anyway.

Alice ran further into
the wood and came upon a
caterpillar making smokey
vowels.

"Who are you?" he
asked, puffing out a 'U'.

Alice blew away
the smoke ring around
her head—and blew the
caterpillar right out of his clothes!

Alice was worried until she saw that the caterpillar had become a butterfly.

The new butterfly told her, "One side of the mushroom will make you grow taller, and the other side will make you grow shorter."

With that, he flapped his new wings and flew off into the sky.

Alice broke off two pieces of the mushroom. "I wonder which side is which," she said. With a shrug, she bit into one of the pieces. She soon found out which piece it was.

Alice sprouted up through the trees and caught an angry bird's nest in her bow! She had to get back to her normal size quickly! She bit into the second piece, then just licked the first piece. Normal sized once more, she put the mushroom in her pocket.

As she carried on through the wood,
she searched for some signs of the White
Rabbit. She did find signs, but they didn't
help much. Just then, she heard singing.
Alice looked up and saw a grinning
Cheshire Cat.

"If you'd really like to know," he said, "the White Rabbit
went that way." The Cheshire Cat tipped his brow. "Of course, if
I were looking for a White Rabbit, I'd ask the Mad Hatter. Most
everyone's mad, here."

Alice walked on until she heard more singing. That must be the Mad Hatter, she thought. She saw him sitting at the end of a long table, with the March Hare.

As the tea-for-twosome wished each other 'Merry Unbirthday', Alice tried to join them. But the pair started shouting, "No room! No room!"

"Oh I'm very sorry," said Alice, "but I did enjoy your singing."

"You enjoyed our singing?" said the
March Hare.

"What a delightful child!"
exclaimed the Mad Hatter. They sat
Alice at the table and offered her tea.
The Mad Hatter swept off his hat
and wished Alice a 'Merry Unbirthday.'
There, on top of his head, was a 'Merry
Unbirthday' cake!

Alice blew out the candle on top of the cake and made a 'Merry Unbirthday' wish.

As if in answer to Alice's wish, the White Rabbit appeared.

"I'm late! I'm late!" the White Rabbit cried.

The Mad Hatter and the March Hare decided that the White Rabbit's watch must be broken, so they decided to fix it with lemon and jam!

Alice shook her head and walked away. "I've had enough of this nonsense," she said.

Alice walked for a while, but couldn't find the path back through the woods. "I wish something here would make sense!" she said to herself. This nonsense world wasn't right for her at all.

Above her, Alice heard the Cheshire Cat again.

"I want to go home," Alice told him. The Cheshire Cat opened a door in the tree. Alice stepped through, into the world of the Queen of Hearts.

The White Rabbit raced past her into the Royal Court. Perhaps, thought Alice, this was why he was always in such a rush. He wouldn't want to be late to announce the Queen. No-one would.

"Her Imperial Highness!" called the White Rabbit, "the Queen of Hearts!" The cards cheered as the Queen entered.

The Queen spotted Alice. "Why, it's a little girl! Now where are you from, and where are you going?"

Alice curtseyed, and answered, "I'm trying to find my way home."

"Your way?!" the Queen shouted. "All the ways here are my ways!"

The Queen calmed down when she learned that Alice played croquet. The Queen loved croquet, and the cards always made sure that she won.

The Queen chose a bird to play her shot
with and prepared to swing. Suddenly,
the Cheshire Cat appeared! Only
Alice could see him.

"You know," he said to Alice,
"we could make her really angry."

"Oh no!" cried Alice. "Stop!"
But it was too late.

The Cheshire Cat tangled the
Queen's skirt, and as she swung her
feet tripped over it, and she flopped
down on the ground—with her skirt
flapping up over her head!

The Queen heaved
herself up. "Someone's
head will roll for this!" she
bellowed at Alice. "Yours!"
The little King pulled on
the Queen's skirts meekly.
"Couldn't she have a little trial first?"
The Queen harrumphed, but agreed.
The White Rabbit read the charge: Alice had caused the
Queen to lose her temper.
"Are you ready for your sentence?" the Queen asked Alice.

"Sentence?" said Alice. "Oh, but there must be a verdict first."
"Sentence first!" the Queen thundered. "Off with her head!"
Alice dug into her pockets and found the two mushroom pieces.
She stuck them in her mouth, and grew until she was towering over
the Queen. The King and Queen told Alice to leave the court.
"I'm not afraid of you!" said Alice.

Just then, Alice felt herself shrinking!

"Off with her head!" the Queen shouted once more. The court of cards began to close in on Alice.

"I simply must escape!" said Alice, and ran away as fast as she could. She ran though a maze, and began to retrace her steps, back through the woods, and soon found herself back on the beach in the middle of the Dodo's race!

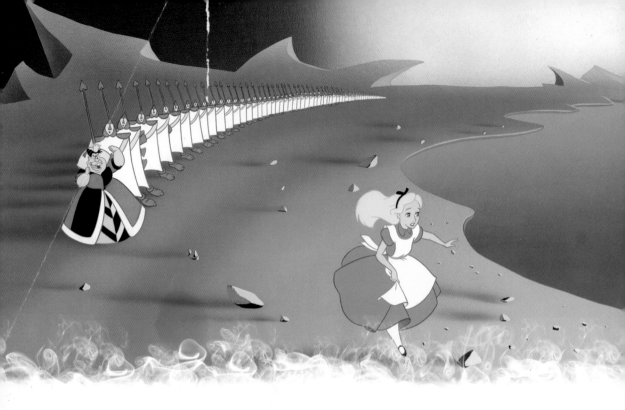

The cards chased Alice down the beach. Through the wisps of smoke, Alice saw the Doorknob and his little door again. She tugged on the Doorknob.

"I must get out!" she gasped.

"But you are out," replied the Doorknob. Alice peered through the keyhole. There she was, asleep in the meadow!

"Alice!" her sister woke her. Alice looked around. The Queen—and her wonderland—were gone. Alice sighed. This day was simply too splendid for nonsense!